I'm Just O.K.

Tara Michener

AuthorHouse™
1663 Liberty Drive
Bloomington, IN 47403
www.authorhouse.com
Phone: 1 (833) 262-8899

This book is printed on acid-free paper.

ISBN: 978-1-7283-7021-7 (sc)
ISBN: 978-1-7283-7022-4 (e)

Library of Congress Control Number: 2020915224

Print information available on the last page.

Published by AuthorHouse 08/21/2020

authorHOUSE®

For Cannon

How are you **feeling**?

Just o.k.

Are you Happy?

Are you MAD ?

I. AM. JUST.

O.K

Are you Sad ?

I'm <sniff>

Are you *Hurt* ?

I'm

Are you

Tired

?

I'm
<yawn>
<snuggle>
just
OK

I have another question...
What does the feeling of o.k. look like?

hmmm...
I dont
think I'm
just
o.k
anymore.

Oh, what emotions are you feeling?

Let me think about it.

I am feeling
Thoughtful.

I am feeling

Enlightened.

I am feeling

Curious...

About what?

feelings.

Tell me more.

Can I have more than one feeling at a time?
Sure. Why not?

Oh good!
I am
feeling
Happy.

Grateful...

Relieved...

and

<yawn>

Tired.

up
up
up

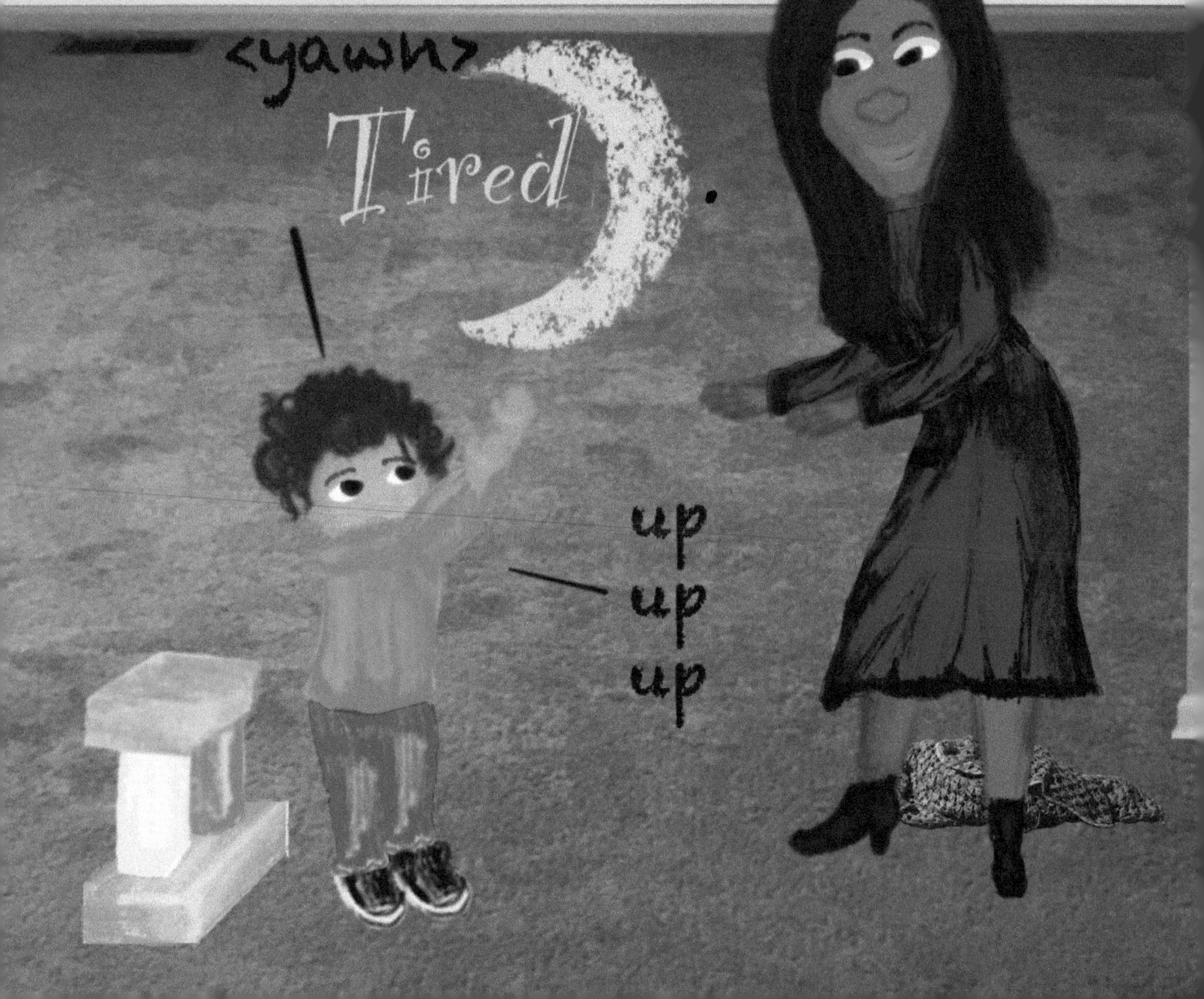

May I have my blanket?
I'm feeling Cold.

Sure.

Here you go.

ununununu

Thanks.

Mommy,
I am
feeling
Content.

Now I'm feeling...

Yes?

That's o.k.
You can tell
me tomorrow.

Mama's baby boy
brings his mama joy...

ZZZZZZZ

Tara Michener loves writing books, eating Twizzlers and drinking Diet Coke... but most of all she enjoys helping people in her job as a Licensed Professional Counselor. She lives in Michigan with her son Cannon and her husband Jason.

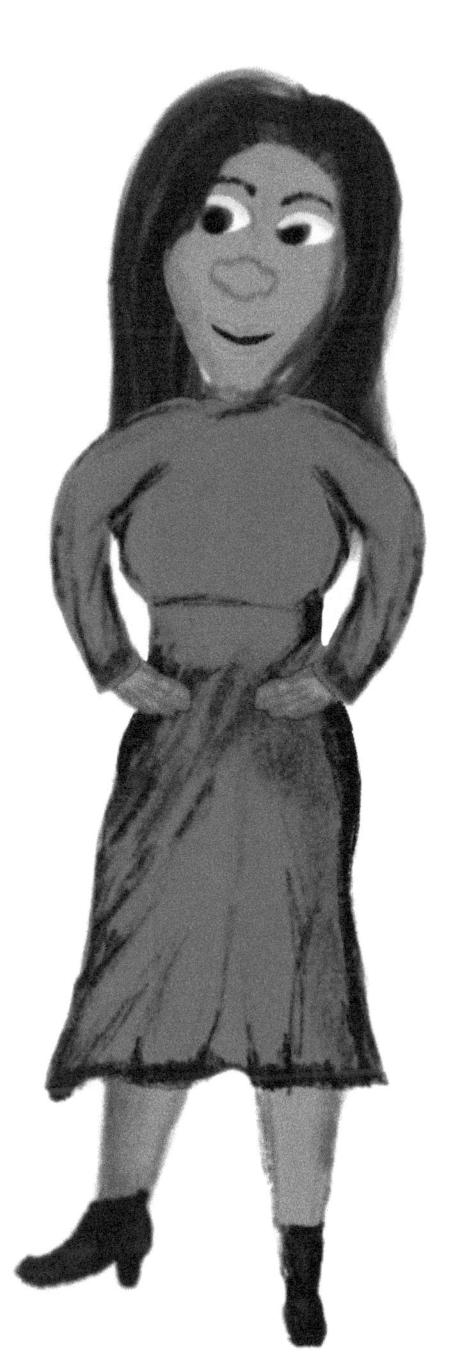

Have you seen her other books?

Who I Am Not What I Am
100% Real
Summer Camp Survival
No Longer Besties: And Other Assorted Teenage Drama
Teen Life Crisis

CPSIA information can be obtained
at www.ICGtesting.com
Printed in the USA
BVHW020348050920
588205BV00017B/990